WELCOME TO PINE RIDGE

Miranda Furness is coping with both the grief of losing her husband and the shock that her family are bankrupt. With four daughters, who no longer have marriage prospects, she knows she must do something drastic, if they are to survive.

An advert for mail order brides seems to be the hope she needs.

However, when they arrive in Pine Ridge, South Dakota, it seems that they have been lied to. Instead of loving husbands, that they can choose over time, they are to be auctioned to the man with the most money.

When the local pastor and a wealthy rancher intervene and rescue them Miranda is still worried about their future. What does Alex Westerman want from them?

Have they jumped out of the frying pan, into the fire?

Find out if Miranda and her four daughters can find safety, love, and happiness in this exciting new series from Indiana Wake & Belle Fiffer.

Each book is a complete and family friendly story and can be read alone, but we hope you will enjoy them all.

Find out about new releases, get special offers, and receive 3 free books by joining my exclusive newsletter http://eepurl.com/gP7I6n

CHAPTER ONE

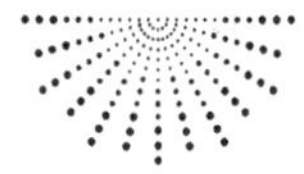

"Would you like some help, Mother?"

Miranda looked up to see her youngest daughter in the kitchen doorway. Smiling, she put the rolling pin down and wiped her floury hands on her apron.

"Karen! I didn't know you were coming over."

"Jacob, Ed, and Brad are planning on doing some Christmas shopping on their own, so they asked us to make ourselves scarce with the children." Karen accepted her mother's hug warmly. "I thought I'd come up and see how you were getting on."

"I'm doing fine." Miranda gestured at her surroundings. "Lucy and Tanya are always on hand, and Debbie is popping in and out all the time. Even though you're all married now, you still come by to help."

"What can we say? Now we've had a taste of how things are, we don't want it to stop because we got married. Besides," Karen smiled and placed a hand on her belly, "I wanted to tell you the good news."

Miranda stared. "What? You're pregnant?" The joy filled her so much that she felt young again.

"I am. Apparently, I'm about four months along. I didn't notice anything different until I was really sick last week."

"That's when you got dizzy at the barn dance, wasn't it? I did get worried about that." Miranda knew a beaming smile was splitting her face. "Why didn't you tell me last week? Surely, you were told then?"

"Sort of. Jacob and I wanted me to rest and soak in the news before we told anyone. My sisters don't know yet."

"So, I'm the first."

Karen nodded. Miranda squealed and hugged her daughter again.

"I'm so happy for you, darling. Another grandchild for me? Between the four of you, I'm going to end up with a little army."

Karen laughed.

"Careful, Mother! Jacob said he always wanted a big family, but I'm not keen on having my body go through childbirth too many more times. The men have it easy, I'm the one who has to carry the children."

"It's not so bad." Miranda patted her own stomach. "Sure, you end up being a little soft around the middle, but that's nothing you can't handle. If your body is strong enough, you'll be able to withstand it."

"Not if the horror stories Lucy has told me are anything to go by."

Karen shuddered. Miranda knew how terrified she was of pain. She squeezed her daughter's hand.

"You'll be fine. I'll be right there if you need me as well. You don't have to worry about a thing."

"I don't know about that."

"I do." Miranda tugged Karen towards the table. "Come sit down and talk to me. I'm making a pie, and I have to roll out the crust."

"I can help with that."

"No, you don't need to worry about anything except keeping me company." Miranda picked up the rolling pin again. "I'm fine I just need someone to talk to."

"What about Alex? You often talk to him, don't you?"

Miranda paused. She didn't want to discuss Alex. The man was insufferable, and he knew it. However, he could kiss really well. It had been two months since the kiss at Debbie and Darren's wedding, and Miranda could still feel the taste of his mouth on hers. The fact she could still remember the kiss left her shaken.

She chose her words carefully. "We don't really talk, Karen. We just end up fighting."

"No, you don't. I've seen you talk to him plenty of times before. You can have a decent conversation with the man."

"Not lately." Miranda slammed the rolling pin down. "We barely talk nowadays. And if we do, it's to argue."

Karen snorted. "Mother, honestly. When are you and Alex actually going to say something about how you feel?"

"Excuse me?"

"It's obvious that you two have feelings for each other."

Miranda froze. Her heart felt like it was stuttering. How did her daughter know? She tried to be nonchalant as she continued rolling out the pastry.

"We don't have feelings for each other. There's nothing there."

"You do realize that nobody believes you, Mother. My sisters definitely think something is there. And looking at how you're reacting right now, I'm certain of it as well."

Miranda didn't like how astute her children were. She had raised them to be intelligent, shrewd women, but she didn't like it turning back on herself. She shook her head and tried to concentrate on the pastry.

"Seriously, Karen, you and your sisters are overthinking it. I have respect for Mr. Westerman for what he's done for us, but that's it. However, he frustrates me more than anyone else."

"I think he frustrates everyone, it's a regular thing," Karen commented. She regarded her mother thoughtfully. "We're not going to be upset if you think about yourself now."

"What are you talking about?"

"You wanted us to be married and have husbands who will love and care about us. We won't be upset if you end up with that for yourself?"

Miranda frowned. "Karen, this isn't a subject I wish to discuss. Besides, there's no one I really want to consider marrying."

That was a big lie, and Miranda hoped that Karen didn't think too much about it. She really didn't want to discuss Alex, or how she wished that she could swallow her pride and admit that she had fallen for him a long time ago. But there was still a small part of her hanging onto her husband. Then there were the circumstances that had led her to this point. That was something that was going to hover over them.

Alex had been kind enough to let them stay, but Miranda still felt like she had been bought.

Footsteps sounded behind them, and Miranda turned to see Andrea, Alex's daughter, walking into the room, heaving a big sigh as she went to the sink and picked up a cup. Miranda rolled her eyes and got back to her work. Andrea had been wandering around the house, very despondent, for quite a while now. It was getting ridiculous.

All over someone she couldn't have in the first place.

"How long until dinner?" Andrea asked.

"Probably about an hour and a half once I get it going." Miranda brought a tin over and put the flat piece of pastry into it. "It won't be long."

"I suppose I can wait." Andrea sighed again. "Although I don't think I'm going to be very hungry when it does happen, so just make a small portion for me."

Miranda didn't respond. She knew Andrea was going to want her to ask why, when she had known for a long time. Andrea wanted to marry Darren, but Darren had never cared for her. Instead, he had married her own daughter, Debbie, and since then Miranda had seen Darren smile more, and his confidence had grown. Debbie was looking equally happy, although she was probably calming down a little. That was a big relief, especially after she had tried to herd cattle on her own; and ended up injured. Miranda dreaded to think about what could have happened.

Miranda shuddered, she had been close to a herd of cattle, but with a fence between her. They were huge and seemed to have little sense when they were spooked. Debbie had finally learned her lesson, and Darren was keeping her happy. They were a good pairing, and Miranda couldn't think of anyone better than the pastor for her high-spirited daughter.

The problem was coming from Andrea. The girl had, for some reason, wanted to marry Darren. She had declared her love for him quite a few times despite Darren saying the feelings were not reciprocated. She had tried to keep Darren and Debbie apart, but that hadn't worked. Now Andrea just wandered around her father's house, sighing heavily and lamenting about not having Darren around her. It was getting annoying. Even Alex was getting fed up with it.

"I hope I have an appetite soon," Andrea went on, sipping her water. "I don't want to fade away to nothing, but I can't bring myself to eat anything."

"You'll eat what you're given," Miranda said sharply, focusing on pressing the pastry into the tin. "You're not going to starve while you're here."

"You would starve as well if you were lovesick."

Karen rolled her eyes. Miranda understood the sentiment, but she didn't stop working.

"Andrea, being heartbroken is hard to deal with. I've been there myself. But wandering around and asking us what love is and how it could betray you is getting silly. You need to accept that Darren is married now, and he doesn't want anything to do with you." Miranda continued with her work hoping that this would work.

"You just don't want Darren to be with me so your daughters can have husbands. If your family hadn't come here, I would be married to Darren by now." Andrea sounded like she was sulking. "Why did you and your daughters have to come here and mess everything up?"

Miranda knew she had been dealing with a short temper the last few days, but now it was so close to snapping. She slammed the rolling pin onto the table, making both young women jump, and swung around on Andrea, who was staring at her in slight bewilderment. Did she not think Miranda was going to snap at this?

"Look, Andrea, I'm not having this. I'm trying to do my job, and that is difficult when you keep going around making comments about my family. Even if we weren't here, you wouldn't have gotten married to Darren. He really doesn't care about you, and lamenting about someone you could never have in the first place is just making you look and sound rather silly. Just go away if you can't say anything that isn't moaning about your current predicament. It's not going to turn things around to what you want, and it's annoying to listen to."

Andrea's face had gone a little pale. For a moment, she looked stunned at the idea that the housekeeper had scolded her. Then her eyes narrowed.

"What's wrong with what I'm saying? I'm allowed to express an opinion."

"You've been expressing that opinion for two months now! The woman Darren married is my daughter, and you've been disrespectful towards her. How about you stop being such a moaning Minnie and accept that we can't always get who we want in life?

Miranda knew she was going to get a conversation with Alex about this - even though he wasn't happy about it, either, Andrea was still his child - but she didn't care. She just wanted it to stop.

Andrea's lips pressed tightly together. Then she slammed the cup onto the table, spilling water everywhere. She sneered at Miranda.

"You don't get to tell me how I'm allowed to feel," she hissed. "Your bratty daughter swooped in and took my man from me. If anything, you should be apologizing for what she did."

"Why should any of us apologize for that? I don't get in the way of love, and you shouldn't, either."

Andrea snorted. Then she stormed out of the kitchen.

Karen watched her go and arched an eyebrow at her mother. "I don't think she's going to let you scold her go that lightly."

"I know." Miranda turned back to prodding the pastry back into the tin. "But I can handle it. After raising four daughters, it's nothing I can't deal with." However, the last thing she needed was more disapproval from Alex. Though she kept a smile on her face her own heart tumbled, just a little.

CHAPTER TWO

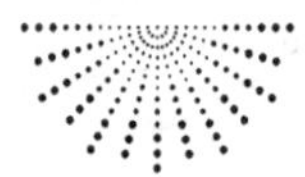

Alex's head was hurting. He tried to concentrate on what he was doing, but it just wasn't happening. His mind was in too much turmoil.

It had been like that since Darren's wedding. When he had broken his own rule about how he behaved with the servants, he had kissed Miranda. That kiss was still firmly on his mind, and Alex couldn't shake the glorious feel of it, or how good it felt to hold her, even for just a moment.

What had happened to his sanity? When Alex rescued Miranda and her daughters from Jago, he said that he was trying to be a decent person and look out for women who desperately needed help. That they didn't deserve to be auctioned off like they were cattle. They didn't deserve to be pawed or leered at. All he wanted to do was give them a proper start in their new life, to give them some freedom to choose for themselves.

Yes, that was all true but there was more. Alex had been lying to himself since the beginning. He had taken one look at Miranda, and something had shifted inside him. Alex knew he wouldn't be able to sit back and let her walk away. He tried to cover his feelings by saying he was being a good person when the reality was he wanted Miranda for himself. He had always wanted Miranda for himself!

And the fact he had actually turned into one of the lecherous men who were trying to buy a bride made him feel nauseous. He had pushed himself onto her. Miranda didn't deserve that from him. If she wanted a new husband, that was for her to decide, not him. The least he could do is give her a job and a place to live so she had less to worry about. And so she didn't have to be concerned about her daughters.

However, all this time, Alex had wanted to tell Miranda the truth. He wanted to confess how he felt and to stop dancing around the topic as he had done for the last year and a half. But if he did, Miranda was going to leave. Alex would be very lucky if she didn't run away after what he had done.

The problem was, that the tension between them was getting too much for him. Alex had tried to keep his distance and remain somewhat standoffish towards Miranda so she wouldn't figure anything out. He knew she didn't really trust him and that she suspected ulterior motives, and she would be right. It was best to leave her dislike for him alone.

Then they had to kiss, and Alex's resolve had almost snapped. What was he thinking when he did that?

"ALEX!"

Alex looked up. Jacob was in the doorway, watching him in bemusement. Alex sat up, rubbing his hands over his face.

"Jacob. How long have you been standing there?"

"A little bit. I think I said your name three times, you only responded when I shouted."

Alex hadn't noticed. He had been wrapped up in his own thoughts. With a sigh, he beckoned Jacob to come in.

"Come on in. What are you doing here, anyway? I thought you were meant to be out on the range."

"I moved things around, to take the day off." Jacob leaned on his crutches as he came in. He was smiling. "Karen wanted to tell her mother about the pregnancy."

"Pregnancy? You're going to be parents?"

Jacob beamed. Alex found himself smiling as he stood up and came around the desk, grasping Jacob's hand.

"Congratulations, Jacob. That's great news. I know you said you wanted a family."

"That was before I lost my leg and became as I was." Jacob shrugged. "But Karen's presence made me change my mind. I can't see anyone but her being the mother of my children."

"She's been a good influence for you, I take it?"

"You could say that. I didn't think anyone would tolerate me or want to be around me, but Karen is... well, she's special."

Alex could attest to that. Out of the four Furness daughters, the youngest, Karen had been the one he was most fond of. She was kind and gentle, a calming presence. She had been more than prepared to look after Jacob after he ended up losing a leg in that landslide. What had really impressed him was that she had done so without any complaints. Alex had been surprised that she would do that to a stranger.

But after seeing how Karen and Jacob were together, it all made sense and that was why it had worked out. Both of them deserved some happiness, and Jacob definitely needed a good presence in his life.

"Miranda's going to be pleased," Alex said, moving around the desk to sit down again. "She loves being a grandmother, even if she complains that she feels too young to be a grandmother."

"She just loves babies. I've heard her telling Lucy she loves to cuddle babies, just as long as she can give them back afterward."

Alex smiled.

"That sounds about right. I know exactly how she feels."

"You never thought about being a grandfather, then?"

"The only way that's going to happen is if Andrea gets married and has children. She's my only child, and nobody is willing to marry her right now." Alex shrugged. "I don't think she'll want to marry anyone anytime soon, given how hung up on Darren she was."

"I was surprised at that. I didn't think she and Darren were remotely compatible."

"You know what Andrea's like, Jacob. If she wants something, she absolutely has to get it."

That was what annoyed Alex. There was nothing wrong with being strong and assertive, but Andrea used it in the wrong way. Her mother had said she could have anything, and anyone, she wanted, and Andrea had taken that to heart. So when something happened that wasn't a part of what she wanted, Andrea got really upset about it. Her behavior was almost like a spoiled child, having a tantrum. It was rather embarrassing.

Alex had tried to get her to back off and be more realistic, but Andrea refused to do it. It was why they had been estranged for some time; Alex wouldn't pander to Andrea's requests. And he certainly wouldn't force Darren to marry her when he loved another.

"I'm sorry to say it, but your daughter is weird, Alex," Jacob said, hobbling over to a chair and sitting down, propping his crutches up against the desk.

Jacob's face dropped, he realized he had said the wrong thing and he was waiting for Alex to tell him off. Alex assessed his feelings. What did that make him feel?

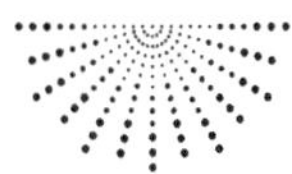

CHAPTER THREE

For a moment Alex said nothing. He knew that as a father he should be angry but he had to admit that Jacob was right, Andrea was strange, and hearing it made him feel nothing. He loved his daughter but he had given up on trying to change her, all he could do was try to minimize the damage she did. "You don't need to tell me, Jacob. I know she is."

Jacob looked as if he breathed a sigh of relief. "And this thing with Darren… I couldn't see it working. Andrea didn't have what was needed to be a pastor's wife. She would have been miserable, even if she wanted Darren."

Alex shrugged. "Andrea hadn't thought that far ahead. I had told her myself that I didn't think she would be right for Darren, but she refused to listen."

"Debbie is a better fit for him."

"She's strong-willed and stubborn, much like Andrea." Alex smiled.

"But Debbie is also sweet and caring. She wants to help people and is more than willing to be what Darren needs in his life. She's willing to bend to what is required of her. Andrea would never bend unless it's to what she wants." Jacob tilted his head to one side. "Even you know that, Alex."

Alex did know. His own wife had been like that. It was no wonder that things had been tense at the end, or that Andrea had turned into the spitting image of his wife.

He did love his daughter. That was never changing. But he was getting fed up with her attitude and behavior. Especially in the last couple of months since Darren had gotten married. Andrea had ended up staying with him in spite of Alex initially telling her she was not permitted on his property; seeing her so down and withdrawn had worried him, so he had allowed her to temporarily move in. Now he was beginning to regret it, especially with the way Andrea was towards Miranda.

He knew the two of them didn't get along, and he wasn't expecting them to be friends. But Andrea was not very respectful towards Miranda, which left Miranda's temper on a short fuse. They were always arguing when Andrea ended up in a combative mood. When she wasn't wandering around the house with a sour look on her face, sighing heavily and lamenting about her lost love.

Alex began to regret helping his daughter out, he had been foolish to think that she needed her father.

"I'm sure she'll find someone who would be better suited to her than Darren." Alex shrugged, did he really believe that? "I don't know what was going on in her head about him, but it will pass. Someone more appropriate will marry her, and then she'll be happy."

"Just as long as he's got lots of money and lots of patience."

"I know she's my daughter and I shouldn't think like that, but you're right."

Jacob chuckled. "At least she'll be able to find happiness. We all need that at some point. Including you."

"Me? I'm fine as I am." Alex felt a touch of heat hit his cheeks. That was ridiculous, how could a man in his 50's be blushing?

"I doubt you are."

Alex frowned. "Of course, I am, Jacob. If I'm destined to be single for the rest of my life, I'll take it."

Because the thought of being with someone who isn't Miranda doesn't sit well with me.

Now you're beginning to sound like Andrea with her obsession over Darren.

"There's nothing wrong with finding someone else. Even Miranda's apparently getting involved."

"What?" Alex frowned. "What are you talking about?"

"I heard about it in town. Apparently, a man has been going around talking about how Jago's snagged himself a beautiful woman, and Miranda has been mentioned by name."

Alex sat up, his heart was hammering against his chest. "I beg your pardon? Someone has been going about saying Jago's courting Miranda?"

"It would seem so."

Alex was confused now. Miranda hated Jago for what he had done to her and her daughters. The last time they had been around each other, Miranda had actually given him a verbal lashing. It had been bad enough that Alex had flinched.

Now she was courting him? She can't have forgiven him for this.

"That... that can't be right. Miranda hates him." Then Alex remembered something else. "Also, isn't he on the run? He was found to have been the bandit stealing from everyone over the last couple of years, I thought he'd gone to ground."

"He hasn't been seen in Pine Ridge. But someone mentioned that one of the townspeople had to be feeding him information and helping him out in hiding." Jacob paused. "After a while, Miranda's name came up. To the point, people believe it. Karen's tried to stop the rumors, but they're spreading faster than they can be quashed."

Alex felt like he was hearing things. Miranda had said a lot of things about Jago. Why would she suddenly consider him for courtship, especially now he was a fugitive?

"This doesn't make any sense."

"That's why I wanted you to know. Sheriff Nelson has heard the rumors, and he wants to talk to Miranda about it. If she does know where he is, she could get arrested for aiding and abetting him." Jacob shook his head. "I didn't know what to make of them until Karen pointed out how stupid it would be. But you need to know about this. If Miranda does know where Jago is…"

Alex didn't want to hear anymore. The thought of Miranda helping Jago in any capacity made him feel nauseous. He stood up. "I'm going to find her. Hopefully, she can give me some answers."

"And if she's innocent and this is a vicious rumor?"

Alex didn't respond. But he hoped and prayed that it was just a rumor. It had to be, no way would Miranda court Jago.

CHAPTER FOUR

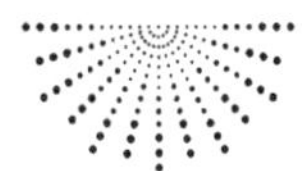

$\mathcal{M}$iranda could tell that something was wrong the moment Alex entered the kitchen. She didn't even need to look around to know he was there; she could feel the hairs standing up on the back of her neck. The tension in the air was more than usual though. The man was like a mountain cat, poised to pounce, waiting for the right moment. What was wrong?

Turning, Miranda saw him filling the doorway, watching her with a blank expression. He looked tense.

Had Andrea gone to him to complain about how Miranda had spoken to her? She wouldn't be surprised that Andrea had gone to him, but she would be if that was the reason Alex was here. Maybe she deserved to be told off for it, but Alex knew his daughter and he didn't often pay attention to her arrogant behavior.

Or it could be because Jacob had just told Alex about the rumors in town about her and Jago. Karen had mentioned it to her, as she had been concerned. There was no reason to be worried, not when it came to Jago, but it was still upsetting that people actually believed it and carried on the gossip. A shiver ran down her spine. The very thought of being nice to Jago was too much. Also, Miranda hated gossip; it was why she mostly kept to herself now.

"Can I have a word, Miranda?" Alex asked. He glanced at Karen. "In private?"

"I... sure." Miranda turned to Karen. "Can you give us a moment?"

"Sure." Karen eased herself out of her chair, touching her mother's arm. "Jacob and I will wait until you're done. Just let me know."

Somehow, that felt like Karen was offering her something, just in case. Miranda gave her a small smile.

"I'll be fine. Off you go."

With one last glance at her mother, Karen left the kitchen.

Alex waited until her footsteps died away before closing the door and turning to Miranda.

"Jacob's just told me something rather disturbing," he said and he was wringing his hands in front of him. "I was hoping you would be able to shed some light on it."

"Let me guess." Miranda went over to the sink and washed her hands. "Someone's been going around saying that Jago has been courting me and that I know where he is."

"Do you?"

Miranda spun around and stared at him. "What?" How could he? "Do you think I know where that man is?"

"Well, do you?"

"Of course, I don't. Why would you even think that?" Miranda wiped her hands on her apron. "You remember what he did to me and my daughters, don't you? After all, you were the one who got us out of that mess. Why would I want to help him, or have anything to do with him, in any capacity?"

"I just have to check." Alex folded his arms. He was still scowling. "If people in town are discussing it, I need to find out for myself what's going on."

"So, you decide that instead of going by your knowledge and experience of me, and what you've witnessed? Instead of trusting me, you're going to accuse me of helping a fugitive?" Miranda shook her head. "Nice, Mr. Westerman. You really have your priorities straight when it comes to me."

"This isn't something to scoff at, Miranda. Sheriff Nelson wants to talk to you about it."

Miranda blinked. "He wants to do what?"

"It may be a rumor, but any lead is good enough."

"It's not even a lead! Someone's messing around!"

"If they are, we won't know until it's been confirmed. And Sheriff Nelson is eager to have Jago arrested, so I can't exactly stop him if he wants to talk to you."

Miranda felt like she hadn't woken up this morning, and that this was just a weird dream. She advanced on Alex.

"I've worked for you since you rescued us, and while I have my own opinions about you, I've never done anything to betray your trust. Add to that the way Jago used me for his own gains, why would I suddenly want to help him?"

"As I said, it's gossip we need to address."

How could he believe this? How could he treat her so badly? Inside, she felt as if her blood was boiling. As if she would explode if she didn't do something. "Well, I've got a way to address it."

Miranda slapped him. The sound of the slap made her ears ring, and Alex's head snapped to one side. Her hand stung, but she was too annoyed to care about that. And she was momentarily distracted by the shocked look on Alex's face. He had not expected her to hit him.

For a brief moment, she wanted to apologize for doing that. But then Miranda reminded herself of what he had just accused her of. Instead of apologizing, she straightened her back and looked him in the eyes.

CHAPTER FIVE

$\mathcal{A}$lex was stunned by the slap but Miranda could still feel her anger desperate for an escape. She prodded a finger into his chest.

"You are insane if you think I've done anything to help Jago evade the law. I don't care for him at all. If I knew where he was, I would have had him locked up a long time ago. He gets no sympathy from me, especially not after trying to sell us off and hurting my daughters."

"Miranda..."

"You are fully aware of that. So why are you accusing me now?" Miranda put her hands on her hips. "Why would you think something so stupid? We may not have been on the best of terms, but I thought you knew me better than that."

"I thought I did."

"So, you're saying you don't believe me?"

Alex swallowed. "I don't know what to believe. People betray others for lesser reasons."

Miranda felt like Alex had slapped her in return. A hard lump formed in her throat. She swallowed it back.

"If you really believe it, you're more stupid than I thought. I would never do that to you, or anyone in my family. Jago tried to use me, and he almost sent Karen off into the canyon and shot Tanya. Do you really think I would be on his side after all that? My daughters mean everything to me. I couldn't be with a man who would behave in such a manner. I could never be with a man who could hurt them!"

Alex didn't immediately respond. He just looked at her, his eyes drifting over her face. Miranda didn't like it when he did this; it made her feel as though her skin was on fire. Alex had that effect on her, and she found it uncomfortable.

Then he reached for her, pulling her off-balance and into his arms. Miranda was about to protest when his mouth silenced her. His arms tightened around her, his lips kissing her until Miranda was breathless.

She should have pushed him away and told him enough. She should have slapped him. But instead, Miranda melted into his arms and kissed him back. It was like her resolve to be angry at him had gone.

Alex Westerman tied her up in knots, and Miranda didn't like it.

When he broke the kiss, Alex was panting heavily. His eyes looked like they were ablaze, looking at her with a heat that made Miranda shiver.

"I hope you're telling me the truth," Alex rasped, slowly releasing her and stepping back, leaving Miranda sway-ing. "Quite a few hearts are going to be broken if you're aiding Jago's escape."

"I... I'm not." Miranda licked her lips. Her mouth had suddenly gone dry. "I would never do that."

"I really hope you mean it."

Then Alex turned and pretty much stormed out of the room, slamming the door behind him.

Her legs feeling weak, Miranda stumbled to a chair and sat down. Her lips were still throbbing from the kiss. It felt like he was still kissing her.

What had just happened there? She didn't know what was going on anymore. Why would Alex do that after everything they had just argued about? Was he trying to make a point?

Miranda was getting a headache trying to figure it out.

"Mother?"

Miranda jumped. Karen was coming into the room. She frowned at her mother.

"What just happened? I heard raised voices."

"I think Alex just accused me of being on Jago's side."

"Seriously?" Karen looked confused. "I would have thought he would be on your side. He always has been before."

"I don't know about that."

"I do. He's always been defending you. Jacob said he needed to know about the rumors in town, but we didn't think he would actually doubt you."

"I'm not entirely sure if he doubted me." Miranda rubbed at her head. The pain was pressing down on her temples. "I can't be around him right now. Not with this uncertainty. But I don't know what to do."

For the first time since they arrived in Pine Ridge, Miranda felt lost and afraid. Somehow, having Alex around actually helped her out in terms of her mood. Even if he drove her mad, knowing he was there made her feel settled and safe. Miranda had never felt threatened.

Now she was floundering for the first time in a long time, and she didn't like it.

"Do you want to come back with us?" Karen asked. "Jacob and I are heading back now, and we've got a spare room. You can stay with us until things have settled down."

"Are you sure?"

"Jacob was the one who suggested it. I agree you need a bit of space from Alex right now."

It sounded like a good idea. But Miranda wished she didn't feel like she was running away from him. However, she needed to get out and clear her head. It would be best for both of them.

She took a deep breath and stood up.

"All right. Just let me get a few things. And I'll tell Alex."

"Jacob can do that. You and I will get you ready." Karen gave her a sympathetic smile. "Things are going to be fine. You'll see."

Right now, Miranda didn't know what to think. She was still rather shaken by Alex's confrontation and his kiss. The two were the total opposite of each other. They had her head spinning and her heart aching. She wanted to talk with him, but she needed to think and breathe properly, and she couldn't do that with him close by.

CHAPTER SIX

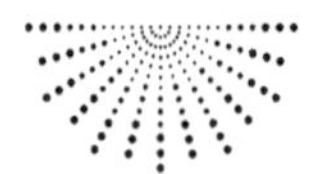

Alex stood at the window and watched Miranda leave on the wagon; Karen was sitting with her while Jacob was upfront. She didn't look towards the house, but Alex could tell that Miranda was upset. He wanted to stop the wagon and hold her, apologizing for the way he had spoken to her.

But he couldn't move. He could only watch them disappear through the gate and around the bend in the road. Then he turned away, slumping onto the couch with his head in his hands.

That hadn't gone well at all. Deep down, Alex knew that Miranda wouldn't have anything to do with Jago. She was far too angry about his actions, and he was aware that Miranda would rip the man to shreds if given the opportunity. But there was a part of him that wondered if it was true. A foolish, jealous part and that part had grabbed hold of him to the point it was starting to seep into him.

Miranda didn't deserve that, and Alex felt ashamed to have said something that accused her of aiding and abetting a fugitive. It wasn't like she had any time to go and be on his side, anyway; nothing was out of place, and whenever she did have time off, it was simply spent with one of her children, who always went with her. If one of them had been aware of this, they would have said something immediately. Especially Tanya, seeing as Sheriff Nelson was now her brother-in-law.

Why did he attack her like that? Alex should have held onto his trust in her and listened to what she had to say instead of talking as if she had done something wrong. He was a fool for doing that.

He also knew why he had behaved the way he did. If he didn't, Miranda was going to get suspicious of him and demand answers. Alex would end up confessing how he felt about her, which would just end up in another fight. And, more than likely, have Miranda leaving him. Alex didn't want that.

You're being stupid. She wouldn't leave you because you're in love with her. That's just in your head.

But is it? Would she stay or would she go?

"Are you all right, Father?"

Alex looked up. Andrea had walked into the room and was watching him curiously. Alex lowered his hands and sat back.

"I'm fine."

"Are you sure?"

"I'm sure. Is there something you wanted, Andrea?"

Andrea pursed her lips. "I was going to see if Miranda could make me something to eat, but she's gone."

"You're a grown woman. You can make something yourself."

"I don't know what I want. And it's meant to be her job."

Alex gritted his teeth. Why did his daughter have to whine?

"Miranda has gone to stay with her daughter for a few days. We're going to be on our own, so you're going to have to get yourself something to eat."

Andrea stared. "But what about the workers? Don't they need someone to feed them? You've lost pretty much all of your servants because you allowed them to get married."

"They can manage to fend for themselves. We managed before, and it's not for very long. Besides, if the Furness girls want to get married, that's up to them. I did say this was temporary, after all."

Andrea snorted and folded her arms.

"I feel like you've been too soft on those girls. They were given a lot of freedom, and now they're off and you have no staff."

"As I said, we can manage. And Miranda isn't going to be away for very long."

A sliver of fear curled in his stomach; that was what he hoped. Although, Alex wasn't sure how long she would be gone. A few days could literally mean a few days, or it could be a week, maybe more. He didn't think he would be able to cope with it.

It was strange how empty the house felt without Miranda's presence. Alex felt lonely for the first time since she had come here with her daughters.

"She probably won't come back at all," Andrea huffed, scuffing her shoes on the rug. "She's going to be sneaking off with her lover, I'm sure of it."

"What are you talking about?"

"I've heard the rumors as well about her and Adam Jago. How they've been sneaking around. I'm sure they've turned into partners in crime." Andrea sniffed. "They'll be gone and away from here before we know what's really going on."

Alex sat up. "Miranda hates Jago. She would never have anything to do with him."

"How do you know? You've only got her word for it."

"Also, partners in crime? If that was the case, why would Jago shoot Tanya and try to run Karen off the road? Wouldn't he want to keep them safe for her?"

"Perhaps she wanted to get rid of them."

Alex felt a wave of anger inside of him that was getting out of control.

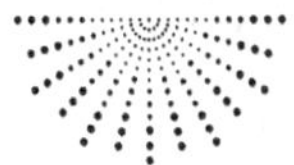

CHAPTER SEVEN

"**A**ndrea!" Alex snapped.

"She might have a life insurance policy on them," Andrea said, she was so enjoying spreading her lies that she hadn't noticed his tone.

"Andrea! Enough!"

"What? It's perfectly possible." Andera arched an eyebrow. "I'm sure you have one out on me. I am your daughter, after all. Or you have one for yourself, just in case."

Alex frowned. "I don't have a policy on anyone. Certainly not me."

"Why not? You should, just in case something happens to you."

"I've got everything in my life sorted should something happen to me. And Miranda is not so cold as to put a life insurance policy on her children and then kill them off. That's the making of a person who's not right in the head."

"Jago more than likely got her to do it. He's always looking for ways to get money off people."

"But to resort to murder?"

Andrea rolled her eyes. "You've been admiring her from afar for too long, Father. You should know that anything's possible. Just like it's possible for Adam Jago to take money off people. It's possible for Miranda Furness to do the same. I wouldn't be surprised if she's a black widow type, either, and that her husband died a bit more suspiciously than she made out."

Alex didn't know what was going on here. Andrea was sounding very bitter. He stood up.

"Why are you talking about Miranda in such a way?" he asked. "What did she do to hurt you?"

"You really don't know what she's done to me?"

"I'm at a loss. I know you two butt heads on occasion…"

"She shouldn't be here at all," Andrea snapped. "She should have stayed where she was, and we wouldn't have this mess. If she had stayed back in her old town with her daughters, then I would be married to Darren by now."

Alex was taken aback. He stared at his daughter. "Are you saying that she's the one at fault for you not marrying Darren?"

"I was getting through to him. And then Debbie Furness came along, and Darren wouldn't look at anyone else. She ruined all my work on getting him to fall in love with me." Andrea pouted. "I love him, and he was taken from me. It's not fair."

Alex was trying to turn all of this over in his head. The mentality of his daughter was really odd.

"It's been two months since Debbie and Darren got married, and you're still upset about it?"

"Debbie is Miranda's daughter, and Miranda decided to come here to start a new life. If she hadn't…"

"What gives you the right to blame Miranda for something that wasn't anything to do with her?"

Andrea huffed. "Seriously, Father, you're meant to be on my side. I am your daughter. Don't you want me to be happy?"

"I want you to be a decent person and not mope around the house wishing for something that can never happen," Alex shot back sharply. "Being grumpy and blaming an innocent person for something that nobody could control is just pathetic."

Andrea's mouth fell open.

"Did you just call me pathetic?"

Alex knew he shouldn't have said that but she was pushing him too far. "You're behaving as such. You're certainly embarrassing yourself." Alex shook his head and stepped around her. "I've got some work to get on with. I think it's best that you pack your things and leave tomorrow. Go back to where you were staying before."

"What?"

"I said you could stay for a while, and now you've outstayed your welcome. It's best for both of us."

Andrea looked horrified. Then she stomped her foot. "That's not fair! I'm your daughter! You shouldn't be throwing me out."

"Not too long ago, you were telling me that I wasn't your father and that I should not consider you my daughter. Now you're wanting me to look out for you because you're dealing with what you call heartbreak? Make up your mind what you really want from me, Andrea, and stick to it."

Alex wasn't about to have more of an argument; he was too emotionally worn out for that. All he wanted was to be left alone. Maybe things would look better tomorrow, he wasn't sure. But he could try.

If he was lucky, Miranda would come back soon. If she didn't...

Alex knew he was going to regret letting his doubts get in the way.

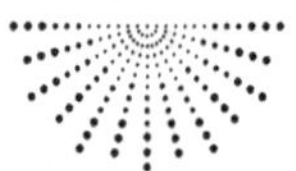

CHAPTER EIGHT

Miranda woke up and lay staring at the ceiling for a while. It took a moment to remember where she was: staying with her daughter and her husband. Just for a few days, and then she could figure out what to do next.

Right now, she was really upset about Alex even slightly doubting her, for him thinking that she could ever be on Jago's side. That would never happen, but Alex seemed to question her. It had never happened before. Even when they were arguing, he never seemed to waver in his trust of her. Yet now, it was like he didn't really know her.

Then again, he didn't properly know her due to Miranda keeping herself from divulging too much about herself.

She had done it in the beginning so Alex didn't use anything against her when she had concerns about his motivations. She didn't trust him then. But after all he had done, and how patient he was with her and her daughters, her trust for him had grown. And then she still couldn't tell him everything without opening a part of herself that she had kept closed off from everyone except her husband.

Even though it wasn't scandalous, sharing anything beyond the superficial things felt too intimate when it came to Alex.

Her daughter, Lucy had teased her about being such a fool and not doing anything about Alex, but Miranda ignored her. There was nothing there. There couldn't be. He was just helping them out, nothing more.

She couldn't possibly be in love with him.

But she was. And it hadn't been a sudden thing that jumped out of nowhere. This had been creeping up on her for a while. Miranda had been aware of how things were whenever Alex was around, and it annoyed her that this was how easy it was to fall into a routine with him. When they weren't squabbling with each other, they worked together really well. Miranda liked that they could fall into something and barely need to ask the other what they should do. Alex seemed to respect her for that.

And yet she couldn't bring herself to accept that there was something between them. Whenever things seemed to get too comfortable, Miranda panicked and turned up the animosity. It wasn't until the kiss that she really explored why she was so responsive towards Alex and why she felt so emotional around him.

Her husband had been the only one who could elicit such strong feelings in her like this. Even though he was now gone, Miranda still felt guilty for feeling something so fierce for another man. She knew it was silly, and that there was nothing to feel guilty about, but she couldn't help it. It was embarrassing.

Hopefully, a couple of days away from Alex could get her thoughts in order, and Miranda would know what to do about what was going on. Right now, she didn't know if she could stay at the ranch, not with the tension between them.

She certainly knew that she couldn't stay if Andrea was there. She was whining and wandering around expecting sympathy for her situation. Making Miranda's life as miserable as she could. It was as if Andrea felt that

Miranda had no right to be happy, simply because she wasn't.

Miranda was getting fed up with the woman for behaving like a brat. Darren was her son-in-law now, and Miranda was fond of him. She wasn't about to have Andrea getting in the way of his marriage. She wouldn't be surprised if Andrea was plotting something to try and break them up.

It was not happening. Not while she was around. Miranda wouldn't allow it.

Rolling out of bed, Miranda splashed water on her face from the basin in the corner of the room. It didn't seem to lift her mood, but it certainly woke her up. She got dressed, catching sight of herself in the mirror. She had dark circles under her eyes, her hair needed a good brush, and she was pale. Not very attractive at all.

What did Alex see in her?

Pushing that thought aside, Miranda grabbed a brush from her bag and tugged it through her hair. Not for the first time, she grumbled about having curly hair that always ended up in knots. Once it was looking vaguely presentable, she pulled it back and used the many pins she had managed to get out the night before to keep it up, twisting her hair into a knot on the back of her head. It tugged at her scalp, but at least she looked like she was ready to step foot outside the front door. Even if she did look a little severe.

Maybe severe was a good thing. Miranda could use the pain to focus herself.

Heading downstairs, Miranda entered the kitchen and found Karen there. Her daughter was stirring something in a bowl at the table. She looked up as her mother came in.

"Morning, Mother."

"Morning." Miranda looked around. "Are we the only ones here?"

"Jacob's gone to work. It's just the two of us right now." Karen peered at her mother. "How are you feeling? Has a night away made things any better?"

"I don't know." Miranda sagged into a chair. She didn't like feeling exhausted so soon after waking up. "Things are just going around inside my head right now, and it's really difficult to get them to stay still."

"Sounds about right, given the circumstances." Karen stopped stirring. "Wouldn't it be simpler to just tell Alex the truth?"

"The truth? About what?"

"About how you feel?"

Miranda groaned.

"Karen, we went through this last night. My answer isn't going to change."

"Why not? Alex deserves to know, doesn't he?"

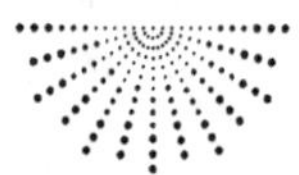

CHAPTER NINE

That idea was foolish. Alex must never know how she felt. "It would just make everything more uncomfortable," Miranda said, why was Karen pushing her? "You think I can just go up to Alex, tell him that I'm in love with him, and expect him to reciprocate?"

"From the way things have been between you two lately, I wouldn't be surprised if he said it back to you." Karen shrugged. "I would actually be surprised if he rejected you."

Miranda frowned. "You're not making me feel any better, Karen."

"Sorry. But never say never. Isn't that what you always said to us?"

"That's different."

"How?"

Miranda groaned and sat back, rubbing her hands over her face.

"I really don't want to go through this again. I just want a few days away from that man and that insufferable woman. If I stay there, it won't be long before I wrap my hands around her throat. I can't stand how she's moaning all the time about her position."

"Is she still whining about not being Mrs. Darren Hunter?"

"Oh, yes, do you think she talks about anything else? You heard her yesterday."

Karen sighed.

"I thought she would accept it and move on. Everyone saw very clearly that Darren didn't even like Andrea. I don't know who got it into her head that she would marry Darren and be happy when she's so disliked, but it's stuck there." She shook her head, absently brushing her hair back behind her ears as she carried on stirring.

"I can't see her being the perfect pastor's wife, anyway. That life and how she demands to live are worlds apart."

"I don't think she was paying much attention beyond Darren's looks. I can't see her being a pastor's wife, either."

"And you can see it with Debbie? After she spent eighteen months demanding to be a part of the men who drove the cattle all over the place?"

Miranda smiled. "She's tenacious. But she loves him and working with him is what she wants. She can adapt to any situation, and I know Darren can temper her stubbornness. He's already mellowed her, and she's done really well so far."

"That's true. Debbie certainly seems calmer. Happier, even." Karen shrugged. "Then again, I guess I can say the same about me. I'm a different person from when we were back where we grew up. I don't want to go back to that."

"I don't blame you. I don't really want to, either." Miranda looked around. "Is there anything I can do around the house? I can't just sit still and do nothing."

"Mother, you don't..."

"Yes, I do."

Karen laughed.

"You spent most of your day organizing the house and making the staff do their jobs. Now you're the house-keeper, and you act like you've been doing it for years."

"Being in charge is what I'm good at. It's not that diffi-cult." Miranda stood up. "So, tell me what I can do."

"Mother..."

"You're pregnant, and while I'm not going to stop you, I can take the heavier loads off you, while I'm here."

Karen looked like she wanted to argue, but she gave in. She gestured towards a basket just inside the back door.

"You can take the washing out and hang it up if you wish. There's not much to do, but the basket is heavy. The pegs are in the bag on the top."

"Not a problem." Miranda came around the table and hugged her daughter. "You don't have to worry about me. Just being here for a couple of days is going to do me a lot of good. And I'm glad I can spend time with you."

"I just want you to be happy, Mother."

"I know. And I am, despite the awful start, coming to Pine Ridge was the best thing we ever did." Miranda frowned. "Although, I'm not too happy about the rumors about myself and Jago going around. I'm still annoyed Alex would doubt me."

Karen bit her lip.

"I'm sorry we caused you problems, but we thought you needed to know."

"You didn't cause problems. Whoever started the rumors caused this."

Miranda really hoped she could find out who did start the rumors. They were going to get a strong verbal lashing from her once she cornered them.

Miranda picked up the basket and propped it on her hip, heading out into the backyard. It was a balmy day, still rather warm for late September. It wouldn't be long before it started getting chilly, and things were going to start shifting. Miranda did like the change in the fall, watching the leaves turn different colors and fall. She especially liked the crunching beneath her feet.

There were a load of trees on the property Alex had. And the previous fall, Miranda had gone wandering through them, feeling like a young girl again when she went to the park. It brought back a lot of memories, although some of them had resulted in her crying.

Alex had found her, and while Miranda was embarrassed about being caught so vulnerable, she appreciated his company. He had simply stood there in silence, waiting for Miranda to calm herself. At that point, Miranda really wanted him to hold her and say it was going to be all right.

It had been the first time in months when she wanted some comfort, someone to make her feel better. And she hadn't been brave enough to ask for it.

Miranda sighed and pushed the thought of Alex away. Right now, she needed to get some focus and take her time away from him. Then she was going to head back and see if she had any courage to confront him about what was going on. They couldn't dance around it forever, especially seeing as Miranda was going to work for him. If they could work past it, then Miranda could figure out how to go forward. If they couldn't...

The only silver lining in leaving was that Miranda wouldn't have to deal with Andrea. The woman was a pain. Alex said the same thing, but he couldn't completely turn his back on his daughter. As a mother, Miranda understood that part.

She went over to the washing lines and put the basket down. Then she began to put out the washing. It wouldn't take long, and then she would go back and see if Karen needed any help. Karen might say she should sit down and put her feet up, but Miranda just couldn't do that. After getting used to being a housekeeper, she couldn't see herself doing anything else.

She had a lot of respect for her former servants now.

Miranda finished putting up the washing on one of the lines, just as the wind picked up. One of the sheets hit her in the face. She tugged it aside, blinking as the wind picked up some dirt and blew it into her face. Wiping her eyes, Miranda made her way back to the basket.

Only to freeze when she saw Jago standing by the basket, watching her with a slight smile on his evil face.

"Nice to see you again, Miranda. I've been waiting for you."

Waking up in the morning, Alex was surprised at how cold and empty things felt in the house. He hadn't noticed that before. Then again, maybe he had, but he hadn't paid much attention to it.

Well, he was paying attention now. And he was painfully aware of it. Miranda's presence had seeped into everything, and now with her gone, things were feeling odd. He didn't like it, he didn't like it at all.

How he hoped that Miranda would come back. If she did, then he would get down on his knees and beg her for her forgiveness. Alex had a feeling that Miranda would enjoy that, seeing as they were often at odds with each other. He was sure she took joy in goading him to frustration. The tension between them fluctuated so much, that he couldn't keep up with it.

It wasn't until he gave in to it, and kissed her, that Alex realized he didn't want to do that anymore.

Then he had to worry about Miranda and the rumors about Jago. The rumors that she was helping the man evade the law. A smart man would know that she wasn't about to do something like that, not after what happened to her family. But he still ended up wondering, and it all went wrong. When he thought about it he understood. How would he have felt if she had accused him of such a heinous act? He would have been devastated. He would have felt betrayed. Why did he do that to her?

Now Miranda was gone. She might have said she would take a few days, but it was going to feel like a lifetime. Alex knew how much he had messed up, knew how much he wanted to apologize, to take it all back. Could he explain to her that his mind turned to mush when she was around? That she messed with his head and had him turned inside-out so much that he made such a huge mistake?

Alex had given up on women, he had decided they were too much trouble and Miranda was trouble, with a capital T. But she was so much more; interesting, exciting, comforting. He missed her so much when she was not here and Alex didn't want to let her go.

Dressing and splashing water on his face, he headed downstairs just as Andrea was coming out of the dining room. There was a pout on her face that a small child would be proud of.

"There's no breakfast," she complained.

"Of course, there isn't. Miranda isn't here." Alex turned in the direction of the kitchen. "We can make our own breakfast."

"What?"

"We're grownups, aren't we? We have hands. It's not going to take much to find something we can eat."

Andrea snorted. "I don't see why we have to do it." A quizzical and calculating expression crossed her face. "Can you make me something as well?"

Alex just ignored her. He wasn't about to treat his grown daughter like a child. Yet again, he regretted allowing her to stay. Once they had eaten, Alex was going to tell her to go back to wherever she came from. They could go back to the superficial relationship they had before.

It was upsetting to know that his only child was not someone he wanted to be around. Alex was sad he couldn't have a close relationship with Andrea. He wasn't really sure where things went wrong, but all he knew was Andrea was not someone he liked to be around. Miranda's daughters had behaved more like his children than Andrea ever did, simply by giving him some decency and respect. Even Debbie had been a delight to live with, despite the fact that they butted heads about what she wanted to do.

It was rather surprising that people he had barely known for a couple of years respected him more than his own child. Then he realized that he loved them like his family. It was a startling revelation and he wondered if he would ever have that relationship with Andrea. Wouldn't that be something?

Entering the kitchen, Alex looked around. Miranda normally made bread every day, so there had to be some around. He didn't need much, just bread and cheese. It was simple, but he was a simple person when it came to food. Unlike some people, he could take care of himself if needed.

There was some bread in a large tin. There was at least half a loaf left. Plenty for both of them today. Maybe he should make some bread once he had checked that all the work on the ranch was being done; it had been a while since Alex had made bread on his own. Sometimes he had some interesting results, but it would, usually, be edible.

He was just cutting the loaf when Andrea appeared in the doorway. She wrinkled her nose when she saw what he was doing.

"Seriously, Father?"

"What? Do you think the bread cuts itself?" Alex didn't look up as he cut himself two slices. "This can keep us going. Unless you want to use those skills you were shown to cook something for us and the workers?"

"No!" Andrea scoffed. "I'm not a servant! I'm not about to cook anything!"

"Miranda wasn't a servant before she came here, and she could cook. It's a skill you should have or if not you should learn."

"Miranda, Miranda. It's always about Miranda."

Alex looked up sharply.

"She's done a lot for my house and my ranch since she and her daughters have arrived. You will not be disrespectful towards her, Andrea."

Andrea sniffed. "It seems like you're more stuck on her than I thought."

"What are you talking about? What do you mean by 'stuck on'?"

"You're in love with her, aren't you?"

Alex straightened up, fixing his daughter with a glare.

"Whether I am or not has nothing to do with how I treat Miranda. I have a lot of respect for her in spite of everything. The least you can do is extend the same courtesy."

"To a servant?"

"To someone who has more decency than you have."

Andrea folded her arms. "You think I'm going to let her sneak into our family, turn your head, and marry you so her daughters can get your inheritance instead of me having it all? Not a chance."

Alex felt his blood run cold.

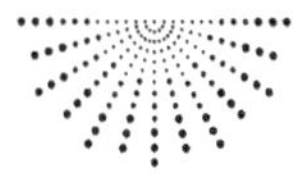

CHAPTER ELEVEN

"That's why you're horrible towards her? Because you think Miranda and her family are going to take my money?" Alex could hardly believe his ears.

"Why else?" Andrea spat at him

Alex stared at her. He had suspected it, but to hear it out loud was just shocking. He was struggling to believe that the woman before him was his own flesh and blood. When Andrea was a child, she had been the perfect daughter. She had never gotten into trouble, and she was always respectful and kind. But as she got older and became a young woman, Andrea had changed. She became a younger version of her mother. Alex's wife had turned into a greedy, mean person as the years went on.

Alex was shocked that he had thought she was a good person. When she died, things had been really bad.

Being a widower had been bearable. Being estranged from his daughter hurt, but he could get through it. But being separated from Miranda, even though their relationship wasn't the one he wanted... that was killing him.

"I can't believe my own child would not want me to be happy," he said quietly. "Just so you can get my money."

"You're meant to pass it onto me when you die. It'll end up getting split between her children and me if you get married." Andrea pouted. "That's not fair."

"Can you just think about me and not my money? I'm not a bank, Andrea."

"Then what else are you useful for? I've been waiting for you to tell me that you'll give me whatever I want, and I was going to say several thousand dollars so I could get myself in order. As my father, you were supposed to give it to me without question."

"You what?" Alex couldn't help but burst out laughing. "Even if we were on good terms, I wouldn't have given you that much. And I would have asked you what you wanted it for specifically."

"You would be stingy even with me?"

"I know what you're like. I want you to be responsible. Someone has to be if you won't."

Andrea scowled. Alex was expecting her to stomp her foot again.

"What's the point in getting rid of Miranda if you're not going to give in to what I want?"

"Excuse me?" Alex frowned. "What did you say?"

It was then that Andrea seemed to realize she had said too much. She gulped and started to leave, but Alex darted around the table and grabbed her arm.

"You are not going anywhere, Andrea. What did you just say? What's the point in getting rid of...?" Then something seemed to click. "Are you saying you started the rumors about her and Adam Jago?"

Andrea didn't say anything, but she didn't have to. Alex saw the answer in her eyes. He couldn't believe it.

"Really, Andrea? You started lies to get me and her to fight?! So that she would leave because I didn't trust her? How pitiful can you get?"

"Pitiful?" Andrea flinched. "How can you call me that?"

"Because you are. I didn't raise you to be a spoiled brat, certainly not at your age." Alex stepped away from her abruptly. "I don't know how you thought this was appropriate, or acceptable. All because you don't want anyone to take away my money?"

Andrea glared at him.

"I'm your daughter, aren't I? That's my money, and that Furness woman's family is threatening my future. What sort of a person would I be if I didn't fight for it?"

Alex shook his head, he didn't know where to start to answer her. "Since when have you wanted to be my daughter?"

He saw the doubt in her eyes and she started to answer but he didn't want to hear it so he cut her off. "I was helping out people who needed someone on their side. If I fall in love with one of them, that's nothing to do with you. You don't have a kind bone in your body, nor any compassion. And to concoct a lie that Miranda is helping Jago to make me doubt her?" Alex paced away, running his hands through his hair. "I think you're going to need to work really hard..." How he wanted to say something mean about where she had stuck her head but he would not stoop to her level. "... to get me to accept you as my daughter. Right now, you will get nothing!"

Andrea's face went white. "Father!"

"What? You don't like me. You show up just to talk about money or how I should use my relationship with Darren to get him to marry you. It was all about your own gains, using me as your father to get what you want." Alex's chest hurt as he kept talking. "I don't know what I did to deserve a child who doesn't care about me except for what I can do for her, but I'm fed up with it, Andrea. I want you out of my house."

"What? You would throw me out?"

"Do you think you deserve respect and attention from me after what you've done?" Alex snapped. "You keep saying you wanted to marry and be happy, but how was that going to happen when Darren isn't rich? Why were you so fixated on him?"

Andrea's mouth opened and closed. Alex didn't want to hear the explanation. He waved her away.

"Just get out of here. I'm going to find Miranda. If you have any sense left, make sure you're not here when we get back."

"But where am I supposed to go?"

"As long as you don't use me, I don't care. Now get out."

Andrea looked like she was going to argue, but she faltered when Alex glared at her. Then she turned and slumped out.

Alex leaned on the table and closed his eyes, fighting back his anger. Knowing Andrea had made up the rumors he almost believed was shocking. She had done a lot of things in the past, but nothing like this.

He had to go and find Miranda and apologize a lot for his daughter's actions. Alex could only hope Miranda agreed to come back. The thought of losing her for good was more than he could cope with.

CHAPTER TWELVE

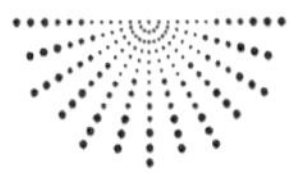

"**W**hat are you doing here, Jago?"

Miranda was surprised she could actually speak. She could feel the fear gripping her, like a steel hand on her gut, from the moment she saw Jago standing there. The man looked arrogant, standing between her and the washing basket, close enough for him to grab her if he wanted. He didn't appear to be armed, but Miranda wouldn't put it past him to be carrying something.

Was he going to attack her? Or kill her? Miranda knew she had to get out of there, but she couldn't move. Her legs wouldn't work.

"I was looking for you, actually." Jago's eyes glinted as his gaze slid over her. "It's not often I find you off Alex's ranch. I'm surprised that you are as well. Did you and Alex have a fight?"

"Why were you looking for me?" Miranda asked, her mind reeling at what he was saying. Had he been watching her? "You and I didn't exactly part on good terms. I seem to remember you threatening me for not going along with your plan."

"Did I threaten you?"

"You certainly did. And you threatened Alex for ruining your chance to get your money. Didn't you get money from Alex when he paid for us?"

Jago snorted. "I was going to get a lot more for all of you, but he ruined it. He just gave me a stack of cash, said the price was non-negotiable and if I chose to argue, he would get the sheriff."

"Sounds like a good idea to me."

Jago bared his teeth.

"I had plans for you and your daughters, and you decided to go with him? Because he had money?"

"He wasn't there throwing salacious comments at us. He was actually someone who wanted us to leave there unharmed. Unlike some people, Alex actually cared."

Jago sniggered. "Oh, really. You think he cares about you?"

"I know he does. He wouldn't have taken all of us away if that wasn't the case."

"Sounds like he had his own plans, and he wasn't planning on cutting me in."

Miranda felt nauseous. Jago really hadn't cared about their welfare. All he saw was money and women who needed an opportunity to get away and start afresh. He didn't care that he was selling them into a worse situation than the one they had left; as long as he got his money, he was happy.

"My daughters and I had lost my husband, and we wanted a new start. You fed into our naivety and our lack of knowledge about how things go, and tried to sell us! We were going to be used, abused, and thrown aside by the men you had picked out!" Miranda wagged a finger in Jago's face, her anger pushing aside her fear. "If you were going to pretend to be a matchmaker, you could at least make a decent job of it!"

Jago grabbed her wrist and yanked her off-balance. Miranda stumbled into him, gasping as she collided against his chest. Their faces were inches apart now, Jago's breath tickling her mouth. He was breathing heavily, and that breath was foul.

"Your daughters had plenty of suitors to choose from, and women are incredibly picky. They find it hard to choose. I just got rid of the indecision. There are so many people here who really want families, and I was giving them what they wanted. You can't begin to imagine how angry they were when Alex came in and got your brats out of there."

"That's not how matchmaking works," Miranda snapped. "And what about me? Were you going to do the same thing with me?"

Jago's eyes drifted to her mouth. He shook his head.

"Actually, I had something different in mind for you. I didn't have anyone to bid on you, even though I had you up there. I thought it would be easier for the five of you to be up on the stage and you wouldn't be any the wiser of what I had planned."

"What does that mean?"

"I wanted you for myself."

Miranda gasped and started to pull back, only for Jago's grip to tighten on her wrist.

"I liked you, Miranda, through our letters. I found you fascinating. Then when I saw you, I knew that I couldn't let anyone else have you. You were mine, as far as I was concerned. I was planning on fulfilling my end of the bargain with the men who bought your daughters, and then I would take you off the stage and say nobody was keen on you, you could have my shoulder as comfort while I consoled you."

"And you would make sure that I was dependent on you while my daughters were abused by their prospective husbands? That I would look to you for everything as you looked after me?"

"Pretty much."

It was so ludicrous that Miranda burst out laughing.

Jago's eyes narrowed. "It's not amusing, Miranda."

"I think it is. What part of your brain thought that was a good idea? Why didn't you just tell me the truth when we met? Also, selling my daughters to men other normal people would call undesirable? That was not going to make me think highly of you." Miranda shook her head. "You really didn't think things through. You didn't make yourself out to be a savior. You just looked like a crook, and a pretty bad one."

Jago's jaw tightened.

"Things are different over here. We don't all come up to the ladies with big flower bouquets and make up many poems to please them. Things are a bit more straightforward out here."

"How is auctioning us off without our consent straightforward? It was cruel!"

"I had plenty of men who wanted to marry your daughters, and I didn't know who to pick, so I decided to open up the field and see who was prepared to spend as much money to get what they wanted."

Miranda felt like she was going to be sick. She slapped him. Jago's head snapped sideways, and then Miranda followed up with a knee to the groin. Jago dropped immediately with a yell, grabbing at himself and letting go of Miranda. Her heart racing, Miranda backed away from Jago before he could grab hold of her again.

"You're a disgusting monster," she hissed. "You try to sell us, attack Karen, shoot Tanya, and you really think I'm going to be with you after all that? You hurt my daughters, and you humiliated me. If I thought you were handsome and fell in love with you after that, there is something seriously wrong with me. You need your head looked at if you thought that was going to work."

Jago rolled onto his side, still clutching at his groin. He scowled up at her.

"You…"

"Go ahead and call me whatever names you want. I'm not having anything to do with you." Miranda pretended to aim a kick at him, which had Jago flinching. "I suggest you either run away before I contact the sheriff, or you stay there and allow yourself to be arrested. You definitely deserve it."

Jago growled.

"You'll pay for that, Miranda. I was doing what I could so you and I could have a life together, and this is how you repay me?"

"You were doing this for me? You've got a strange way of showing it." Miranda stepped around him, heading towards the door. "Follow me, and I'll give you something more to scream about."

She was almost at the back porch when she was grabbed from behind. Miranda screamed and flailed, trying to hit something but failing. Jago's grip around her waist was tight, which made it hard for her to breathe.

"I did a lot of things for you, and you throw it back in my face?" he hissed in her ear. "I fell in love with you last year, and all I get is abuse? That's not happening."

"Let me go!"

"I will. Once we're married. Then you can't run away without my name being connected to you."

Miranda froze. He was actually going to do it.

"Darren will never marry us," she gasped, trying to push his hands away. "He hears about this, and he's going to refuse."

"I never said we would get married here. I'm taking you to the next town, where they don't know us. We'll be married there, and we can start a life there." Jago chuckled. "There, we can start afresh, or even move further west. I've heard the gold rush is still pretty strong along the West Coast."

Miranda really could feel the panic building. She was struggling to breathe.

"My daughters won't let this happen. And Alex..."

"Alex will get over it. And your daughters will know that you're following your heart. They're not your keepers."

"And you plan to be on the run for the rest of your life?"

"Once we're on the West Coast, there won't be any need." Jago kissed her neck. "Then you'll be mine."

Miranda hissed and jerked away, only for Jago to yank her back.

"I will never marry a man like you," she whispered.

"Well, you won't have a choice, will you? Not once the ceremony is done."

"No priest or pastor will allow it to happen."

"You underestimate my abilities to get people to do what I want." Jago started to tug her towards the side of the house. "Let's go. If you scream, I'll make sure something happens to your daughter. We don't want your grand-child to be hurt, do we?"

Miranda stopped struggling as fear seemed to squeeze the life out of her.

CHAPTER THIRTEEN

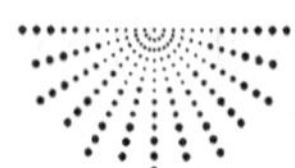

lex heard the shouting as he arrived at Karen's house. One of the voices was Miranda's, and she sounded angry. At least it wasn't just him she was shouting at.

He dismounted, only to see Miranda and Jago coming around the side of the house. Jago had a firm grip on her, and she looked defeated, frightened. This was not like her, he expected her to fight. Alex froze. Jago was here?

Oh, dear Lord, help me. Jago had Miranda.

Miranda saw him first, her eyes widening. "Alex!"

She tried to go to him, only for Jago to haul her back with a snarl. "Don't even think about it. He's not having you."

The sight of his hands on the woman he loved stirred the anger in Alex's chest. He snarled and started forward. "Let her go, Adam!"

"Back off, Alex. Miranda is mine, not yours." Jago smirked as he nuzzled Miranda's cheek. "I saw her first. As far as I'm concerned, that means she's mine."

Alex couldn't believe what he was hearing, and he didn't let it stop him. Anger surged through him, anger and fear, for if he had been just moments later it could have been too late.

He charged at Jago, grabbing at his hair as the other man faltered and yanked him sideways. Yelping, Jago seemed to let go of Miranda because she elbowed him in the stomach and darted out of reach. Alex held Jago's head up, growling into his face.

"Miranda is not going anywhere, and you're absolutely not going to take her. You're going to be held here until Sheriff Nelson comes to get you. We'll be telling him that we've found the fugitive he's been chasing for a long time. Then you're going to jail."

Jago's eyes widened. "No! Just let me go! I'll go! I won't bother anyone!"

Alex didn't see a man in his grip anymore. He saw a coward, a fool who had no guts. He shook his head.

"I don't think so. You'll just come back and do it again."

"I won't!"

"Consider yourself lucky that attempted murder isn't a hanging offense. Then again, you could easily hang from the nearest tree..."

Jago whimpered. Alex had thought it would be more satisfying to catch him, that it would maybe even end with a fight. Hitting this man that had caused so much pain, so much heartache would feel good... but there was nothing.

Sighing, he punched Jago right between the eyes. Jago dropped immediately, lying still on the ground. Alex nudged him, but Jago didn't move. He really was out for the count.

Alex looked up and saw Miranda staring at him. She was a little flushed, there was apprehension in her gaze.

"Is he dead?"

Alex smiled. "No, he's unconscious. But he'll live."

"Are you going to take him to Sheriff Nelson?"

"In a bit. I'll wait for him to wake up, I don't fancy lugging a dead weight." Alex moved towards her. "I've got to do something first."

"What?"

Miranda didn't move as Alex wrapped his arms around her and held her close. She also sighed as he kissed her. It was softer than he had the day before. It was then that Alex realized he was shaking. If he hadn't come along as he did, she might have been gone, and he wouldn't know where to look.

Feeling her in his embrace made him feel better.

Miranda was staring at him when they broke the kiss. "What was that for?"

"I needed to." Alex swallowed. "That scared me."

"It scared me, too" Miranda leaned into him. "He said he was going to take me away and marry me. Then we would go where we wouldn't be found."

"I hope you told him where to go."

"I was in the process of doing that when he threatened my daughters and grandchildren. It shocked me so much. Knocked the breath out of me, but before I could get my fight back, you turned up." She glanced up at him with a slight smile. "But I'm glad you did. You certainly got the point across better than I did."

"I'm glad." Alex kissed her forehead. "Miranda, I'm really sorry. What I did was unacceptable. That was not fair."

"I'll agree with that."

"You're not going to make this easy for me, are you?"

"No. You should know that by now." Miranda shook her head. "You and I butt heads all the time, but I thought you trusted me. Why would you think that I would have anything to do with him?"

The look of betrayal on her face was clear. He had hurt her badly. Was it too late, or could he win her back?

CHAPTER FOURTEEN

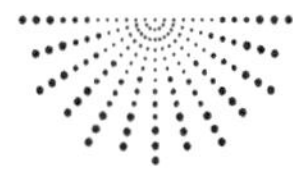

"I just... I guess..." Alex sighed. "I don't know what I was thinking. I trust you, but... there was always that doubt slithering inside of me. And I'm ashamed to say it got me."

"I was going to slap you more than that one time."

"I would have deserved it." Alex hesitated. "I think that I really doubted myself if I was good enough for you and so I was doubting you because... things got so messed up because I don't think straight when I'm around you."

She smiled. "I get like that sometimes. I think it's why I pick fights with you!"

"Aren't we a pair?" He started to relax, maybe he could win her back. "I also found out the source of the rumors. It was Andrea."

Miranda's eyes widened. "What? Andrea? Are you serious?"

"She admitted it herself. She wanted you to leave."

"I get that she didn't like me, but I still don't understand why she would do such an awful thing."

This was going to get embarrassing. Alex slowly eased himself away from Miranda, rubbing the back of his neck. Here it came. It was not how he wanted to tell her, but there was no other way around it.

"She figured out... well, she figured out us... and she didn't want us to get married. She believed that it would mean you and your daughters would end up getting a part of her inheritance, that I would split the money between all of you if something happened to me. Andrea didn't want to share, so she tried to get you to leave so it wouldn't happen."

Miranda was looking at him like he had gone mad. Alex could understand; he was sounding like a fool.

"She didn't want us to... what? Get married? Did she think that was going to happen?"

"Well, all she was thinking about was the money, and the knowledge that I might not give it all to her." Alex spread his hands. "Needless to say, she tried to put doubts in my head that you were helping a fugitive and were romantically involved with another man. I've told her to leave my house, and that she's not welcome back unless she can apologize to you about what she did."

Miranda tilted her head, still staring at him.

"I don't get you at all, Alex. Why did she get the impression that we were going to get married?"

Here it came. Alex took a deep breath. "Maybe because she figured that I was going to ask you to marry me soon."

"What?"

"I've danced around this for nearly two years now, Miranda. I was aware of how wary you were of me, and that your thoughts about my motives were suspicious, so I kept my distance. I put up with your sharp tone and your accusations because I understood it. But I can't keep hiding how I feel about you." Alex was surprised he could look Miranda in the eye as he spoke.

"I... I," Her mouth opened and closed but no more words came out.

"I love you. I always did," he said. "Having you in the house and not being able to say anything because I knew you would refuse me was killing me. But I couldn't let you go. My pride got in the way; I didn't want to be rejected. Having you around was selfish, and yet I couldn't do anything about it because I thought you would tell me to get lost if I told you how I feel." He resisted the urge to shuffle his feet. "Given how you came into this town, I wouldn't have blamed you for being distrustful of me."

Miranda didn't say anything for a moment.

Alex hated that she was silent for this long. Turning away, he checked on Jago. The man was still unconscious, his mouth hanging open. At least he wouldn't be a problem yet.

"You made a complete hash of that, Alex."

Alex jumped and spun around. Miranda was standing directly behind him. Pressing a hand to his chest as his heart missed a few beats, Alex gulped in air.

"You're going to make me drop dead if you keep doing that, Miranda."

"I'm sure you're stronger than that." Miranda smiled. "You'd have to be if you want me in your life."

"What?"

Alex was still stunned as Miranda grabbed his head and tugged him down for a kiss. But he didn't fight it, he was liking how Miranda was in control.

"I love you as well." Miranda's voice was a whisper as she drew back. "But the feelings were strong, and they scared me. I had lost my husband and thought I wouldn't find love again, not at my age. Then I met you, and the fact that I started feeling something was unnerving. I didn't know how to react to it."

"That's why you've been rather brusque with me over the last couple of years?"

"Yes. I didn't think it was right."

"And what about now?"

Miranda bit her lip. "I was going to get you to apologize to me and see if it was sincere, but I think you rescuing me from Jago certainly helped."

"I should do that more often."

Miranda chuckled.

Alex put his arms around her again, still smiling as he kissed her. "You look beautiful when you laugh. I like it."

"You should compliment me more often."

"Just as long as you will give me another chance. That we can start to talk again like we used to. I don't want us to be at each other's throats anymore."

Miranda touched his cheek.

"That's not going to happen, Alex. Not anymore. I love you, I love you so much."

"This love has burned inside of me long and bright, I'm so pleased to finally let it out and I can't wait to spend my life with you." He kissed her once more and she melted into his arms.

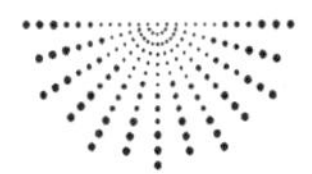

"Do you need any help there?" Alex asked as he came into the room.

"I'm fine." Miranda reached up as far as she could without falling off the chair. "Just a little..."

She screamed as the chair tilted, and then toppled over. She could feel herself falling, only to be caught by Alex. His strong arms wrapped around her, holding her until Miranda got her feet underneath her.

"Would you like to try again?"

There was a hint of amusement in his voice. Miranda thumped his arm.

"I was getting it there. I nearly had the star on the tree."

"And you nearly had yourself in the tree as well," Alex chuckled, kissing her head. "How about you let me do it? I won't topple everything over."

"Are you sure about that? I remember last Christmas when your big feet nearly trampled all the presents."

"Is that why you haven't laid them out yet?"

"I've learned my lesson."

Her husband's eyes twinkled as he kissed her. Then he gently turned her around and nudged her towards the door.

"Why don't you go and check that the turkey is cooking and everything is on schedule? I'll put the star on the tree."

"Why did I have to be the one who plucks and prepares the turkey?" Miranda held up her hands. "My fingers are still feeling numb."

"Because you're better at it than I am." Alex shooed her out of the room. "Besides, your daughters are going to be here soon. Why don't you go and prepare yourself? You're still wearing your apron."

"They won't mind what I look like."

"Our first Christmas as a married couple, and you're meant to be the hostess, not the hired help. Now go."

Miranda rolled her eyes as she left the room, but she couldn't help but smile. There was some bickering still present between the two of them, but it was far more lighthearted.

Ever since Alex pushed his pride aside and confessed how he felt, it was like a weight had been lifted off Miranda's shoulders. Things were better around the house. She still carried on the duties of a housekeeper while being a wife, but Miranda liked it. She liked to be kept busy, and it made her feel fulfilled.

And she also liked being able to cuddle her husband in front of the fire every evening. That was definitely a good perk.

Now they were going to celebrate Christmas as a married couple, along with Miranda's daughters. The two of them were going to host a much bigger family, now that all of Miranda's children were married and there were a few more children. It was going to be busy.

This certainly felt better than the Christmases before her first husband died. Miranda had found it to be rather clinical and staid. Everything was for show, not for fun or pleasure. This was far from staid, it was alive and vibrant and filled with joy.

Miranda entered the kitchen and checked the turkey. It was cooking away nicely. It wouldn't be long before it was ready. She just needed to get on with peeling the potatoes.

"Is that turkey I smell?"

Miranda spun around. Andrea was coming in through the back door, wearing a thick coat and hat against the snowy weather outside. She dusted the snow off her coat, stamping her feet.

"My, it's cold out there! I thought I wasn't going to get here."

"Andrea?" Miranda glanced towards the door into the hall. "I didn't know Alex had invited you."

"I heard from my relatives that you and Father were hosting Christmas, and I thought..." Andrea hesitated. "I thought this might be a good time to... well, to talk."

Miranda frowned. "Talk? What do you mean, talk?" Her stomach turned, though she hated the thought that Alex and his daughter were estranged, she didn't want Andrea to spoil the day.

"I mean, talk about things going on between us." Andrea took a deep breath. She looked uncomfortable, quite unlike the last time they had seen each other. "Also, I'd like to apologize for how I behaved towards you."

Miranda blinked. Had she heard that correctly? "You're apologizing?"

"I am. I've been living with a distant aunt since Father kicked me out and told me to keep away, and she's... well, to say she's knocked some sense into me is an understatement."

"She didn't hit you, did she?"

Andrea grunted. "She didn't need to. Aunt Lavinia is known for giving verbal lashings that would be considered brutal. She was always incredibly honest, and not afraid to say what she thought. And she was prepared to tell me how much of a fool I've been, especially regarding things with my father."

Miranda felt like this was a trap. She folded her arms. "I know you didn't want my family to be around, but your father and I actually love each other. That can't be stopped because you're upset about it."

"I know, and I understand that." Andrea swallowed. "Aunt Lavinia also told me that my mother was not the best role model to look up to, and I should look in the mirror if I want to see the definition of someone who would wreck a home instead of looking at you. She was quite brutal about it all."

"I can imagine," Miranda murmured. "So, you're back here…"

"I wanted to say sorry to you and to Father. And I want to apologize to Darren for how I behaved." Andrea shuffled her feet. "I had an idea in my head, and I didn't like that it wasn't matching up with reality. If I'm honest, I wouldn't have been a good wife for him. We weren't compatible, but I didn't see it."

"Will you say sorry to Debbie as well for how you spoke to her?"

"Of course."

Miranda wasn't sure what to think about this. Andrea could easily turn this around on them and ruin the day. But she seemed genuine enough, and Alex had told her his aunt was good at scaring people out of their delusions. Which was why he had sent his daughter to stay with her instead of finding someone to marry her. In his opinion, this was better for her.

Deep down, he still loved his daughter and didn't want to sell her off like an animal. He was holding out hope that they could have a decent relationship.

For his sake, Miranda would try. It was Christmas, after all.

"I was just about to start on the potatoes." Miranda picked up a bucket. "Do you want to help? I know you don't like to cook, but I've heard you're pretty good once you get going. And I'm not as fast as I used to be with peeling potatoes."

"Would you like me to help you out?"

"If you don't mind? My daughters are going to be here soon, so I want to get things moving smoothly." Miranda gestured at the oven which held the cooking turkey. "You help me with this, and we can have that ready while you and Alex have a talk. I'm sure he'll appreciate it."

For a second, Andrea didn't say anything. Then she gave a smile that actually reached her eyes and shrugged out of her coat, taking off her hat.

"All right. I don't see why not."

It was a start. Miranda hoped it stayed like this. She had a feeling that she could get on well with her step-daughter if Andrea tried.

And Miranda wanted to try, for her husband's sake. That would really make him happy. That would be some Christmas present.

Miranda hadn't come to Pine Ridge to keep Alex happy. But she had been doing it for nearly two years now. What was a little more time between them now they were married?

For her husband, she would happily do many things.

As they peeled the potatoes they chatted and Miranda was surprised that Andrea was a much-improved person.

Soon, her daughters and their families arrived and the house was filled with laughter and the Christmas spirit.

The laughter of children, the delight of adults. Miranda walked into the room to see Alex and Andrea talking. It looked good, Andrea was smiling and being so nice to everyone. Miranda loved her new life but suddenly it felt complete.

"Merry Christmas, everyone," she said.

A chorus of Merry Christmas filled the room with love.

* * *

If you enjoyed this book you can read the whole series here

Miriam Wiggins inhaled deeply, as she watched the passing trees from the small window of the stagecoach. Looking down at Lucy's head on her chest, she wondered how the other woman didn't hear the rapid sound of her palpitating heart. Miriam ran one hand through her blonde hair, further disheveling it, while she patted Lucy's shoulder with the other. Lucy was already scared as it was, and if Miriam showed any signs of fear, it was going to affect Lucy too. Miriam didn't want that. She had to be strong for both of them. Even if it meant putting on a brave face.

"Miriam?" Lucy called softly.

"Yes, Lucy. What is it?" Miriam asked.

Lucy lifted her head and locked her brown eyes with Miriam's blue ones. Her brown hair was long and straight and had been put up in a bun that was managing the journey much better than Lucy's fine and flyaway hair. "Do you think they will like us?"

Miriam sighed. This was the fear that had kept them both awake throughout the long journey west. Would the men they had been sold to as mail order brides like them? Would they have gentle hearts or would they be as cold as ice? "I think I would prefer they respected us, Lucy. But we can't predict how they will react." *Why had she said that?* Keeping expectations low was a good way to prevent further disappointment, but it would not boost her friend's confidence.

"That is the least I want," Lucy said. "If we are to live as husband and wife, they could at least like us. That way, we'll be comfortable at the very least. How are we going to live with people who don't like us? It'll be miserable."

"We'll know when we get there," Miriam said. "Don't worry about that now. We need to wait and see."

Lucy gently shook her head. "I can't believe Mrs. Lauretta actually sold us as brides."

Lucy's statement made Miriam chuckle. "Really, Lucy? You can't believe it?"

Lucy smiled. "Oh, well, yes, of course, I can." Her slim eyebrows raised on a pale face. "But still, it happened sooner than I thought it would. We weren't any trouble. Why were we the first on her list? I understand that they didn't like us, but they didn't have to make it so obvious. Did you see the look on Ruth's face when our departure was announced? She was smirking."

Miriam smiled. The orphanage had been hard and though she was glad to be out of there it would have been nice to make the move themselves. To have had some control over what happened. Her stomach rolled and her heart beat against her chest like a racing horse, but she must not show her own fear. Lucy had a very good reason to fear what her intended would think. Miriam would do her best to help her friend but she may not be able to. "I knew it was going to happen months ago. Besides, we couldn't live at the orphanage forever. We both turn seventeen in a couple of months. It was time to start thinking of our own path in life."

Lucy harumphed.

"I know, Mrs. Lauretta took care of that for us, so... here we are. We're going to be fine, trust me. Aren't you at least glad we aren't at the orphanage anymore?"

"I should be," Lucy said with a smile. "But I think I'm mostly glad that I'm with you. Thankfully, we'll live in Fairplay together. I don't know what I would have done if Mrs. Lauretta sent us to different towns."

Miriam stroked Lucy's hair and sighed. It was true that no one really liked them back at the orphanage. And it was probably because of this shared adversity that she and Lucy became inseparable, like sisters. The women didn't like Miriam because she wasn't fond of cooking, sewing, or other domestic chores of that sort. They also saw Miriam as unnecessarily difficult, when, in fact, all she did was speak up for herself and Lucy. But Miriam didn't mind that. In fact, she had long chosen to be optimistic and now held the faith that leaving the orphanage was a good thing. She couldn't deny her fear of the unknown, but she would make this work, she would make it better. Once more a sliver of fear stabbed her in the gut. What if life in Fairplay was worse than life at the orphanage?

"Miriam, do you think my intended is going to accept me?" Lucy asked, stroking her elbow. "What if he doesn't want me because..."

Lucy fell silent and her gaze dropped to the nub where her left hand used to be. Lucy was missing a hand.

"Lucy, come on."

"Oh, you know it's something I should be worried about," Lucy said. "I've been bullied half my life for it and I still get bullied. My intended might think I'm no use because I don't have two hands. I should be worried about it, shouldn't I?"

"No!" Miriam groaned. "It doesn't matter. It shouldn't matter. Besides, Mrs. Lauretta would have informed your intended already before sending us to the town. Don't worry about trivial things, just keep an open mind."

Lucy sighed. "She would have told him, wouldn't she?"

"Yes. Now rest. You didn't sleep at all last night because of your worrying and you are at it again. We will soon arrive in Fairplay. I'll wake you once we get there." Miriam gave her a bright smile that she hoped looked genuine.

"Thank you, Miriam," Lucy said, nodding. "We're going to be fine. I'm going to try and be optimistic."

"That's the spirit."

Lucy dropped her head back to Miriam's shoulder and closed her eyes. Miriam stroked Lucy's dark brown hair and stared out of the window. Lucy was subtly quivering, and she let out deep sighs at intervals. Miriam could easily sense her fear and she understood it. She wasn't in a good position to dish out advice or words of encouragement, especially when she had her heart in her mouth. She had learned at a young age not to show fear else she would be deemed weak. But Miriam was scared to bits. She didn't know what to expect in Fairplay. It was the first time that she had left the orphanage and she feared that life was about to get worse.

Lucy slowly began to relax in Miriam's arms, she was starting to fall asleep. They both needed the rest but Miriam decided it was best if she stayed awake. They had been traveling for so long, and soon they were going to meet their intended grooms. Miriam could only imagine what the men looked like, what they would be like. All she knew was a name.

"It'll be fine," Miriam whispered. "It has to be."

* * *

Grab all 30 books in this great value box set for FREE with Kindle Unlimited. Love, Heart, and Family 30 Book Inspirational Collection

Find out about new releases, get special offers, and receive 3 free books by joining my exclusive newsletter

http://eepurl.com/gP7I6n

If you would like to find all of my books, look on my Amazon page

While there, click the yellow follow button for updates.

Beautiful Brides and Bouncing Babies Box Set

The Brides of Broken Bow

If you missed any of this series, all three books are now available.
Each book covers one couple and is a complete story.

God bless,

Indiana Wake

ABOUT THE AUTHOR

Indiana Wake was born in Denver, Colorado, where she learned to love the outdoors and horses. At the age of eleven, her parents moved to the United Kingdom to follow her father's career.

It was a strange and foreign new world, and it took a while for her to settle down. Her mom raised horses and Indiana soon learned to ride. She would often escape on horseback imagining she was back in the Wild West. As well as horses, Indiana escaped into fiction and dreamed of all the friends she had left behind.

From an early age, she loved stories. They were always sweet and clean and, more often than not, included horses, cowboys and most importantly of all a happy ever after. As she got older, she would often be found making up her own stories and would tell them to anyone who would listen.

As she grew up, she continued to write, but marriage and a job stole some of her dreams. Then one day she was discussing with a friend at church, how hard it was to get sweet and clean fiction. Though very shy about her writing Indiana agreed to share one of her stories. That friend loved the story and suggested she publish it on kindle. Together they worked really hard, and the rest, as they say, is history.

Indiana has had multiple number one bestsellers and now makes her living from her writing. She believes she was truly blessed to be given this opportunity and thanks each and every one of her readers for making her dream come true.